Caillou

The Jungle Explorer

Adaptation of the animated series: Sarah Margaret Johanson
Illustrations taken from the animated television series and adapted by Eric Sevigny

chouette   COOKIE JAR

Caillou and his mommy were going to do some gardening. Mommy took out some gloves and a few tools.

"Here, this hat will protect you from the sun," she said.

"I'm ready, Mommy," Caillou said.

"Would you like to water the flowers, Caillou?"
Mommy asked.
Just then, they heard a low rumble and the sun clouded over.
"Looks like it's going to rain so I guess you don't need to
water," Mommy told Caillou. "Why don't you see if
Sarah is outside?"

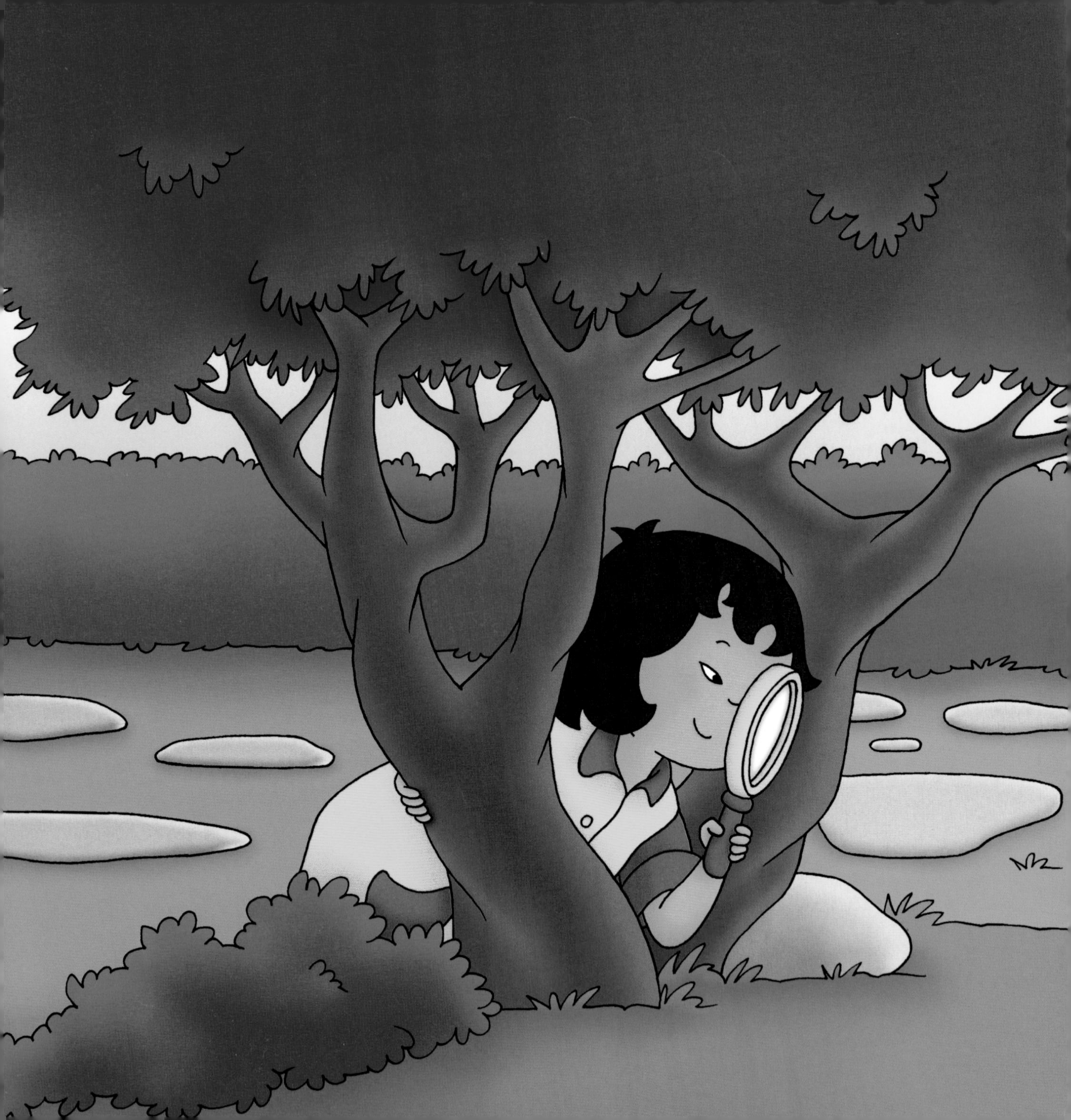

Caillou went in search of his friend
Sarah, who lived next door.
"Sarah," he called out. "Sarah!"
"Hi Caillou," Sarah said.
She was bending over a bush looking
at something.

"What's that?" Caillou asked Sarah pointing to something in her hand.
"It's a magnifying glass," she explained. "It makes small things look bigger."
Caillou looked through the magnifying glass and laughed. It made Sarah's face look much much bigger.

"I have an idea!" Sarah exclaimed. "Let's play 'jungle explorer'!"
"What's that?" Caillou asked.
"We'll pretend we're exploring in the jungle and look at everything with the magnifying glass."

Caillou thought this was a great idea. He got down on his hands and knees to start exploring. "Wow!" he said looking through the magnifying glass at a caterpillar.
"A great big jungle monster!" Sarah exclaimed.

Caillou stood up and looked around. He suddenly saw a beautiful butterfly. When the butterfly landed on a leaf, Caillou examined it with the magnifying glass. "It's as big as a bird!" he said.

The butterfly flew away. Caillou chased it but he got stuck in some bushes.
"The jungle is much thicker here! I don't think I can go on!" Sarah said helping to detangle Caillou.
"I can!" he said, bravely. "I'm not afraid!"
Caillou bent down and crawled deeper into the jungle.

Caillou found Gilbert sleeping in the bushes.
He crept closer and looked with the magnifying glass.
"A jungle lion!" Caillou laughed.
Gilbert woke up startled and ran away.
All of sudden, Caillou heard a very
loud thunderclap.

He called for his friend, "Sarah!"
"Don't worry, Caillou." Sarah said. "That was just jungle drums sending us a message."
"Jungle drums?" Caillou asked.
"Well, they could have been jungle drums but it was probably just thunder," Sarah explained as they left the jungle.

"Mommy, I saw jungle monsters!" Caillou exclaimed. "And we heard jungle drums too!"
Another thunderclap sounded and Mommy said, "Those jungle drums are sending us a message to get inside before we get wet!"

Text adapted by Sarah Margaret Johanson from the scenario of the CAILLOU animated film
series produced by Cookie Jar Entertainment Inc. (© 1997 CINAR Productions (2004) Inc.,
a subsidiary of Cookie Jar Entertainment Inc.).
All rights reserved.
Original story written by Thor Bishopric and Todd Swift
Illustrations taken from the television series CAILLOU and adapted by Eric Sévigny.
Art Direction: Monique Dupras

The PBS KIDS logo is a registered mark of PBS and is used with permission.

We acknowledge the financial support of the Government of Canada through
the Canada Book Fund for our publishing activities.

Canadian   Patrimoine
Heritage   canadien

We acknowledge the support of the Ministry of Culture and Communications
of Quebec and SODEC for the publication and promotion of this book.

SODEC
Québec

Bibliothèque et Archives nationales du Québec and Library and
Archives Canada cataloguing in publication

Johanson, Sarah Margaret, 1968-
Caillou: the jungle explorer
(Clubhouse)
For children aged 3 and up.

ISBN 978-2-89450-724-7

1. Magnifying glasses - Juvenile literature. 2. Science - Experiments -
Juvenile literature. I. Sévigny, Éric. II. Title. III. Title: Jungle explorer.
IV. Series: Clubhouse.

QH278.J63 2009   j502.8'2   C2009-940226-2

Legal deposit: 2009